For Rory – D.M.

First published in 2023 by Nosy Crow Ltd

Wheat Wharf, 27a Shad Thames, London

SE1 2XZ, UK

Nosy Crow Eireann Ltd

44 Orchard Grove, Kenmare

Co Kerry, V93 FY22, Ireland

www.nosycrow.com

ISBN 978 1 83994 597 7 (HB)

ISBN 978 1 83994 768 1 (PB)

A CIP catalogue record for this book is available from the British Library.

Printed in China

Papers used by Nosy Crow are made from wood grown in sustainable forests.

10 9 8 7 6 5 4 3 2 1

Ruffles

and the **cold, cold snow**

David Melling

nosy crow

This is **Ruffles.**

Ruffles **loves** . . .

singing . . .

scratching . . .

eating . . .

fetching . . .

sniffing . . .

chewing . . .

digging . . .

running . . .

and sleeping.

And Ruffles **really loves** playing
with the teeny, tiny kittens.

Today it is snowing,

and the teeny, tiny kittens
want to play outside!

The snow is very, very white
and very, very soft . . .

. . . and **very, very cold!**

Ruffles **does not love** the snow.

It's cold . . . cold . . . cold!

And much too . . . slippy . . . and slidey . . .

 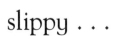 

and **sinky** . . . especially in . . . the **deep snow places.**

But the teeny, tiny kittens **love** the snow!

Until . . .

Plumfff!

Oh dear! Maybe the snow is too deep for the teeny, tiny kittens.

Ruffles can't see **any** of the kittens!
But he can hear them . . .

Miaow!
Miaow!
Miaow!
Miaow!
Miaow!

The teeny, tiny kittens need Ruffles' help!

But Ruffles is scared of sinking and getting **stuck** in the **deep snow places.**

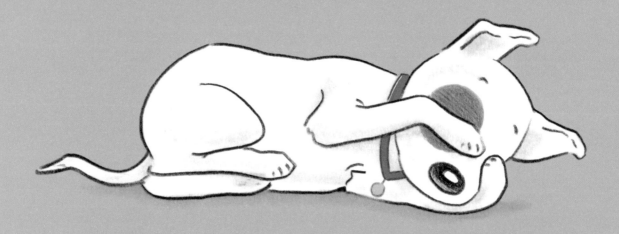

What will Ruffles do?

Ruffles thinks . . .   and puzzles . . .   and worries . . .

and sits . . .   and barks . . .   and whimpers . . .

and runs in circles . . .   then stops . . .   and thinks again.

Then Ruffles is **very** brave . . .

and Ruffles . . .   slowly . . .   slowly . . .

pulls out . . .   one . . .   two . . .

three . . .   four . . .   five . . .

. . . teeny, tiny kittens.

Then Ruffles takes
the kittens all the way . . .

. . . back home.

Ruffles and the teeny, tiny kittens are
safe and warm in Ruffles' cosy, cosy bed.

Ruffles **loves** . . .

singing . . .

scratching . . .

eating . . .

fetching . . .

sniffing . . .

chewing . . .

digging . . .

running . . .

and playing in the **not** too deep snow.

But most of all, Ruffles
loves helping his friends . . .

until it's time for a **new** game!